The Littlest
Lighthouse
Keeper
to the
Rescue

Heidi and Daniel Howarth

QEB Publishing

Henry lived in a lighthouse and
helped the lighthouse keeper.

One night, he couldn't sleep. It was a very noisy, stormy night.

In the morning, Henry opened
his porthole and looked out.

The stormy night had turned
into a lovely, sunny morning.

But what was that noise?
Someone was crying.

From high up in the lighthouse,
Henry couldn't see who it was.

Grabbing his cap, he scampered
down the stairs to find out.

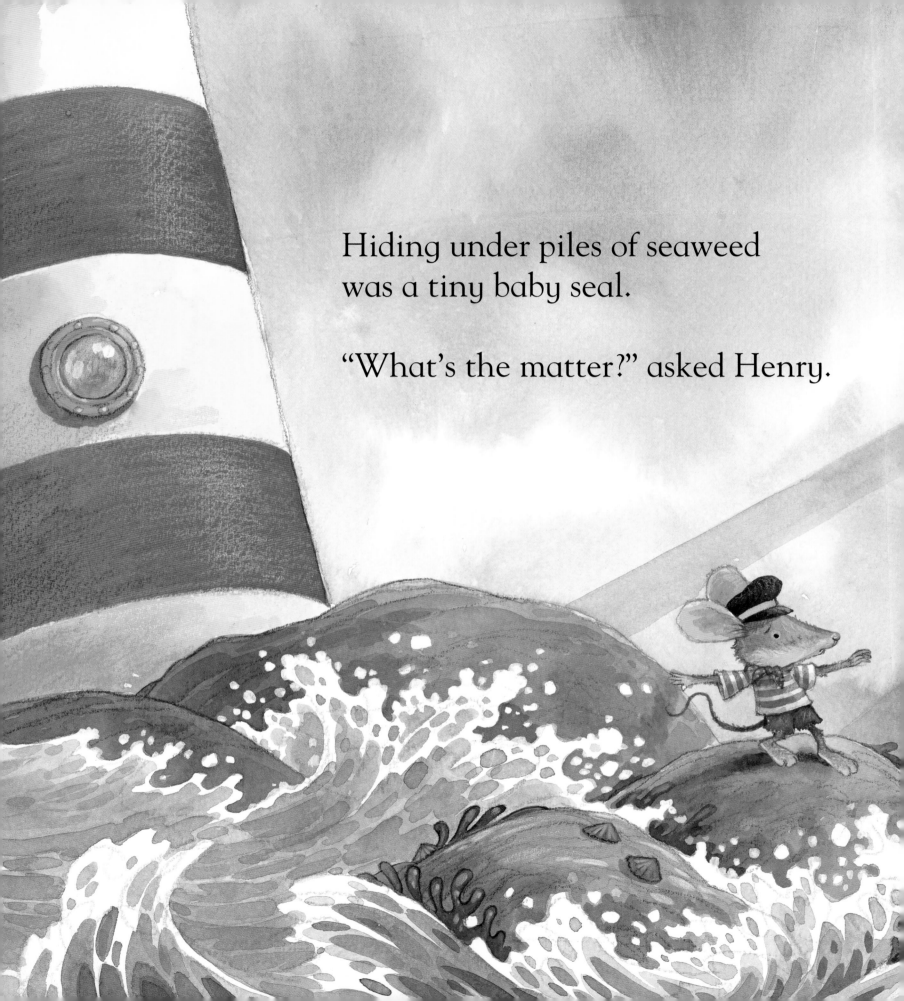

Hiding under piles of seaweed
was a tiny baby seal.

"What's the matter?" asked Henry.

"I was washed up here by the storm," cried Baby Seal.
"I'm very hungry and scared.
I want to go home."

What would Baby Seal eat?
Henry tried his favorite foods.

Cheese...

Cake...

Chocolate…

Baby Seal didn't like
any of them and just
cried louder.

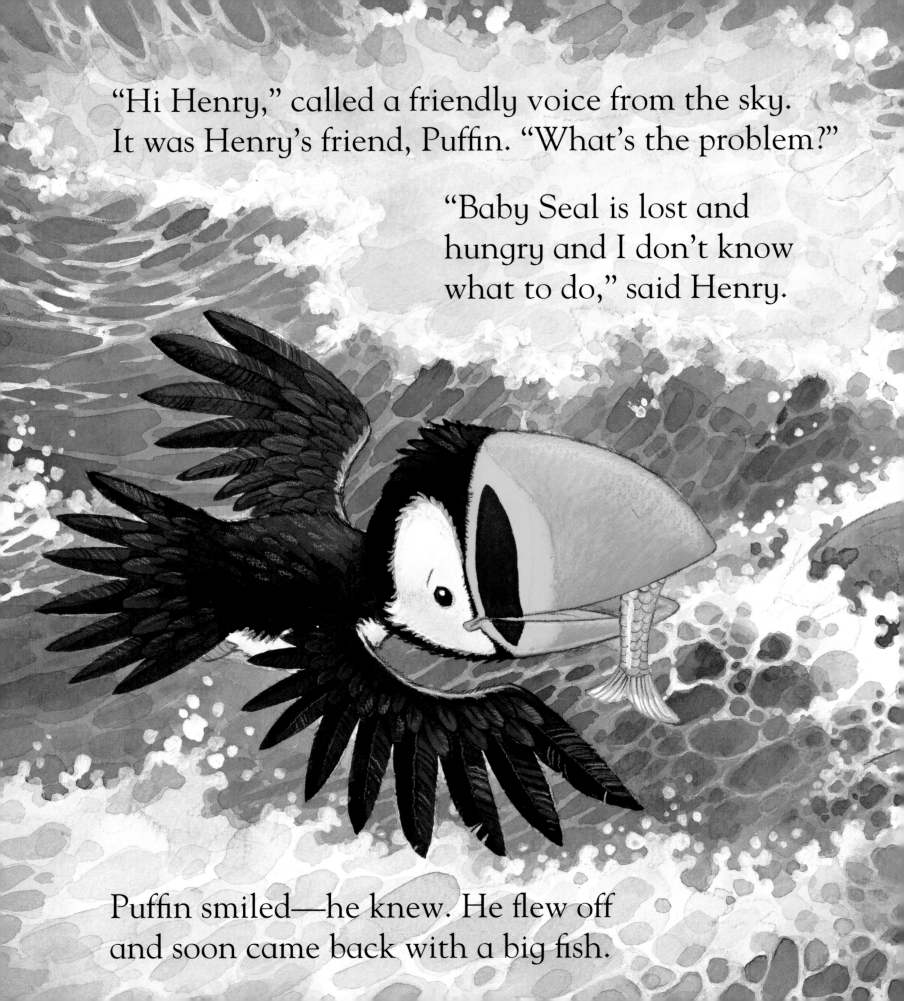

"Hi Henry," called a friendly voice from the sky. It was Henry's friend, Puffin. "What's the problem?"

"Baby Seal is lost and hungry and I don't know what to do," said Henry.

Puffin smiled—he knew. He flew off and soon came back with a big fish.

Baby Seal gobbled it up and stopped crying. Then they all agreed to search for Baby Seal's mother.

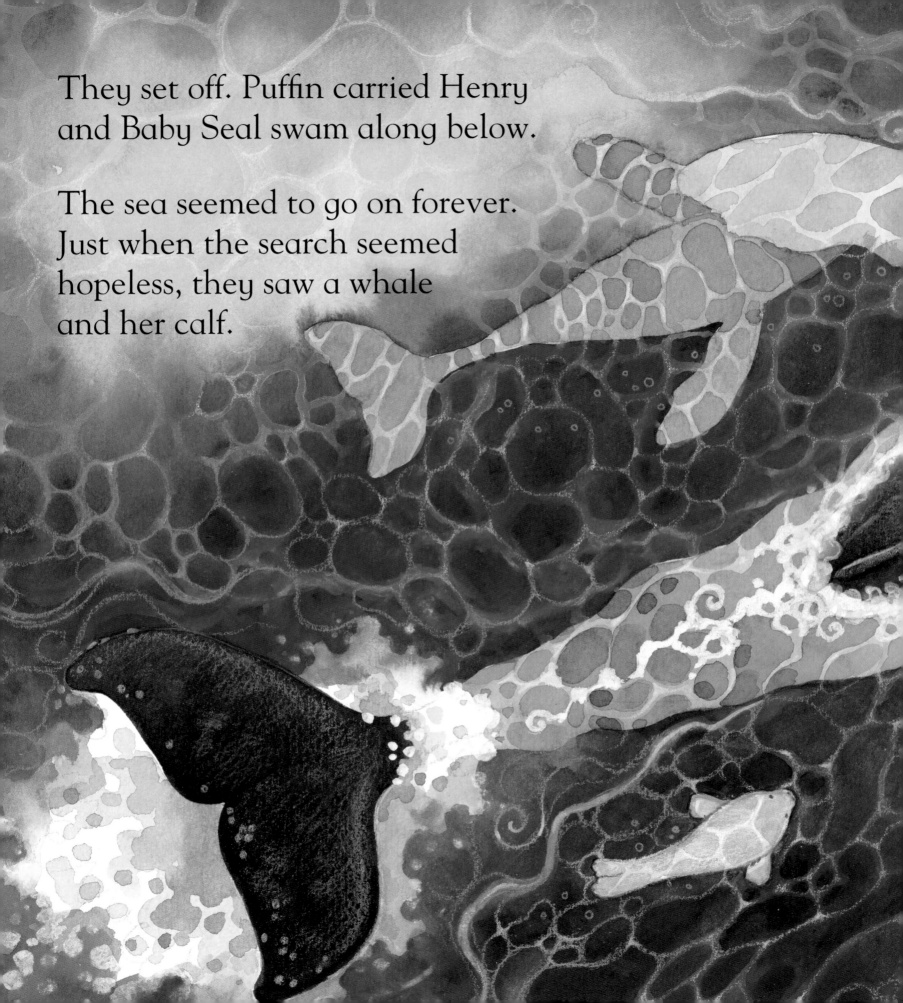

They set off. Puffin carried Henry and Baby Seal swam along below.

The sea seemed to go on forever. Just when the search seemed hopeless, they saw a whale and her calf.

"No, sorry," puffed Whale. "Have you asked Albatross?"

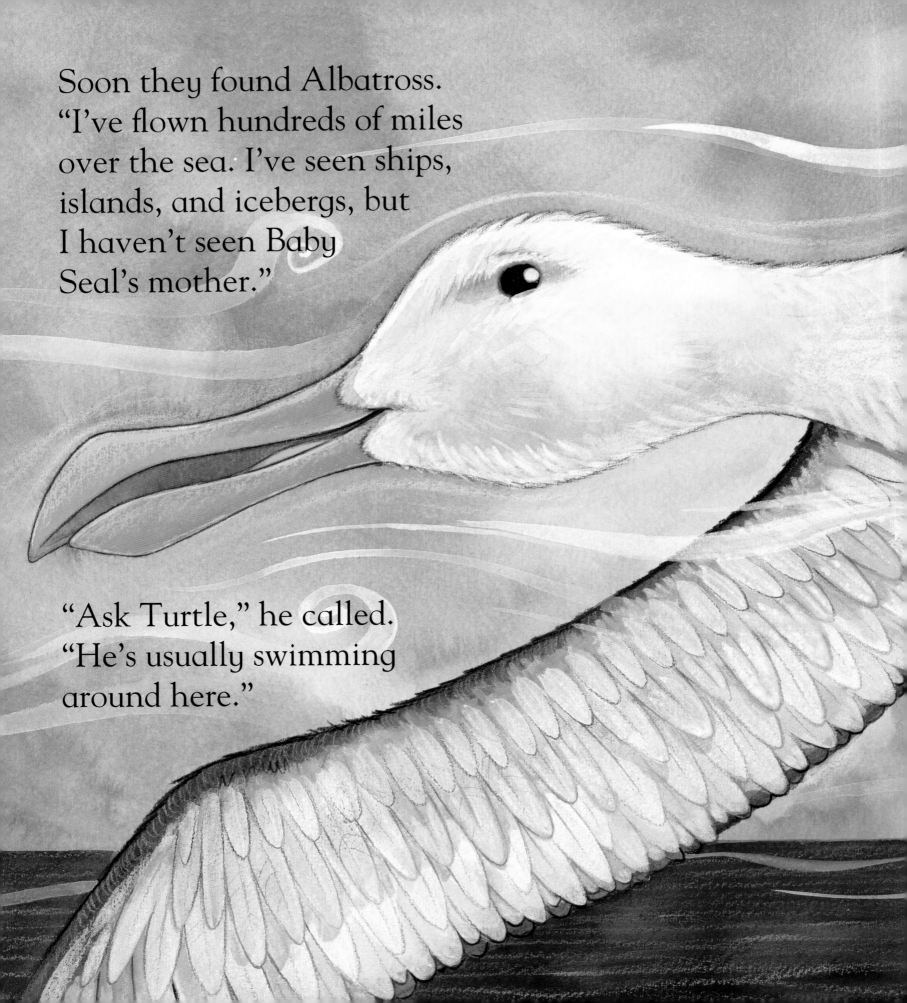

Soon they found Albatross. "I've flown hundreds of miles over the sea. I've seen ships, islands, and icebergs, but I haven't seen Baby Seal's mother."

"Ask Turtle," he called. "He's usually swimming around here."

Turtle was sad to hear about lost Baby Seal.

"Sorry, I can't help," he spluttered. "I missed the storm. We were following the jellyfish from warmer seas. I did meet some dolphins who'd been in the storm. You could ask them."

Henry was fed up. They had
searched all day and hadn't
found Baby Seal's mother.
They were very tired. As the
sun began to set, they sat
on a buoy for a rest.

"You all look a little sad," called a
friendly voice. "What's wrong?"
Henry told Dolphin about
lost Baby Seal.
"I've seen Baby Seal's
mother!" Dolphin cried.

Henry, Puffin, and Baby Seal followed
Dolphin all the way back to the coast.
There on the rocks were some seals.

"Can you see her? Is she
there?" asked Henry.
Baby Seal shook her head.

They moved a little closer. "How about now?" Henry asked. Baby Seal shook her head again.

Baby Seal didn't see her mother, but her mother saw her.

She raced over to give Henry
and Baby Seal a big hug.
"Thank you for bringing my
baby back!" cried Mother Seal.

Back at home in the lighthouse, Henry had no trouble sleeping that night... no trouble at all.

Notes for parents and teachers

- Before starting to share this story with children, look at the front cover and help them to read the title. Can the children guess what the story is about and where it takes place?

- Henry lives in a lighthouse. Do the children know what a lighthouse is and what it is for? Explain what lighthouses do and where they are built. Have any of the children seen a lighthouse? The light can only be seen at night and when there is a thick fog. There is also a loud fog horn to warn the ships. What do the children think a fog horn would sound like?

- When Henry finds Baby Seal, he doesn't know what she eats. His friend Puffin knows. What did Puffin bring for Baby Seal? Is there anything else she might like to eat?

- Henry and Puffin meet a whale, dolphin, and turtle in the sea. Can the children think of other creatures that live in the water?

- Ask the children to draw pictures, using the pictures in the book to help them, of a whale, turtle, and smiling dolphin. Do dolphins really smile, or do they just look like it?

- Do the children know how big an albatross is and how far it can fly? What does it eat and where does it build a nest for its eggs?

- Ask the children to make a play of the story. Some of them can be Henry, Puffin, and Baby Seal. Others can be the other characters in the story. What would they talk about and what sort of voices would they have?

- Seals live in the sea, but they can also come out onto the land. Can seals breathe underwater? Discuss how they keep warm in very cold water and how the mothers look after their babies.

- In the story, Baby Seal gets lost in the storm. Happily she finds her mother again with the help of Henry and Puffin. How do the children think it would feel to be lost? Would they know what to do it they got lost?

- Henry and Puffin are good friends and like helping anyone in trouble. Ask the children to talk about their friends. Can they think of a time when they helped someone? What did they do and how did they feel?

Copyright © QEB Publishing, Inc. 2009

Published in the United States by
QEB Publishing, Inc.
3 Wrigley, Suite A
Irvine, CA 92618
www.qeb-publishing.com

Library of Congress Cataloging-in-Publication Data

Howarth, Heidi.
  The littlest lighthouse keeper to the rescue / by Heidi Howarth ; illustrated by Daniel Howarth.
    p. cm. -- (QEB storytime)
  Summary: Henry, a mouse who lives in a lighthouse, seeks help from a puffin and other animal friends to find the mother of a very hungry baby seal who was separated from her mother during a storm.
  ISBN 978-1-59566-753-3 (hardcover)
  [1. Lost children--Fiction. 2. Seals (Animals)--Fiction. 3. Marine animals--Fiction. 4. Lighthouse keepers--Fiction. 5. Mice--Fiction.] I. Howarth, Daniel, ill. II. Title.
  PZ7.H83592Lit 2010
  [E]--dc22

2009001996

Printed and bound in China

Author Heidi Howarth
Illustrator Daniel Howarth
Designer Alix Wood
Project Editor Heather Amery

Publisher Steve Evans
Creative Director Zeta Davies
Managing Editor Amanda Askew